ANOTHER PURPLE CRAYON ADVENTURE

HAROLD'S
ABC

STORY AND PICTURES

by
Crockett
Johnson

📚 HarperCollins*Publishers*

Copyright © 1963 by Crockett Johnson
All rights reserved. Printed in the United States of America
For information address HarperCollins Children's Books,
a division of HarperCollins Publishers,
195 Broadway, New York, NY 10007
Library of Congress catalog card number: 63–14444
ISBN: 0–06–443023–5 (pbk.)

14 15 16 17 18 PC/WOR 10 9 8 7 6 5 4 3 2

Harold decided one evening to take a trip
through the alphabet, from A to Z.

D

To go on any kind of trip he had to leave home. He started with A for Attic.

And he left his yard, taking his purple
crayon and the moon along.

To get very far he was going to need a lot of words. B is for Books.

He could find plenty of words in a pile of
big books. He was ready for anything.

Harold was always ready for something to eat. And C is for Cake.

He took a large cut of cake and ate it as
he continued on his way.

The cake made him thirsty, and he wanted
a drink.   Luckily D is for Drink.

He drank right out of the dipper. He was eager to get on with his excursion.

He visited an enormous edifice, the tallest building in the world.

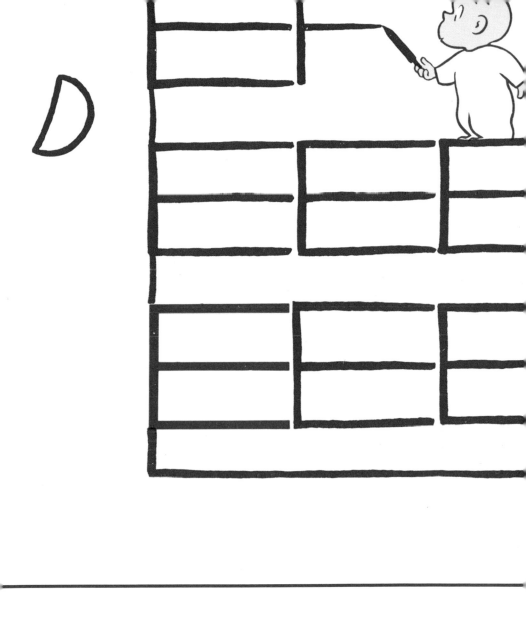

It went up and up and up, floor after floor,
etcetera, etcetera.   E is for Etcetera.

Elevators take people up and down in big buildings, but Harold didn't like them.

They made his stomach feel funny. He went up, over a hundred stories, in his own way.

At the very top Harold was surprised to
see something higher than he was.

It was only the next letter of the alphabet,
flying from the roof.   F is for Flag.

Now he had to get down. G is for Giant.
One happened to be passing by.

Giants generally aren't so genial. But this
one grinned when Harold landed on him.

Harold explained he was in a hurry. The giant gently set him on the ground.

He hastened along. H is for Horse. One
way to go fast is on horseback.

Unfortunately the horse didn't turn out to look much like a real horse.

It made a rather good hobby horse, but a hobby horse doesn't go anywhere.

Harold had to think of some other way to speed his trip. I is for Idea.

He went to work on the next letter with
his purple crayon.   J is for Jet.

In a jiffy he had a speedy little jet plane
ready to take off.

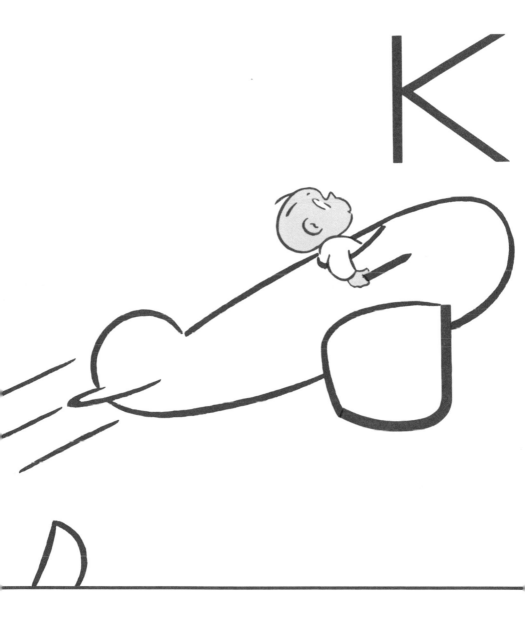

Harold hopped into it and rocketed away.
It overtook the next letter in no time.

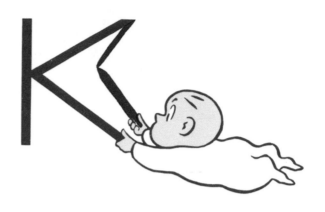

Harold jumped out and grabbed on,
thinking hard of a word for it.

K is for Kite, flying on a string.   Harold
began to climb down the string.

Suddenly a quicker way of getting down struck Harold.

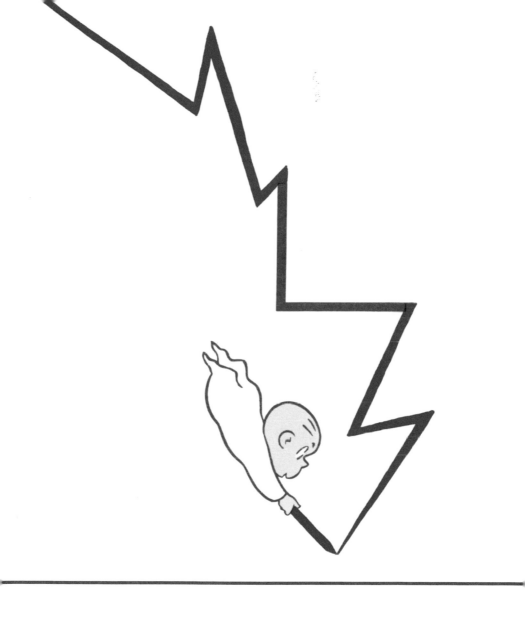

L is for Lightning. Harold held tight to
the purple crayon, going like a streak.

He landed on a pair of tall peaks, high and
lonely. M is for Mountain.

He looked for somebody to ask where these mountains were. N is for Nobody.

Off in the sky he saw an orbiting object.
It looked like a strange planet.

O is for Ours. Our earth! The mountains
were on the rim of the moon.

He looked over the edge, at the side of
the moon he had never seen.

Down below him was the next letter of the
alphabet. Taking aim, he jumped.

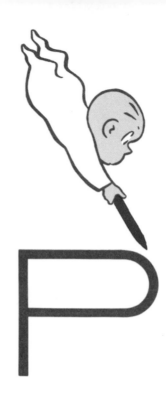

P is for Parachute, he said as he plunged to a plain on the far side of the moon.

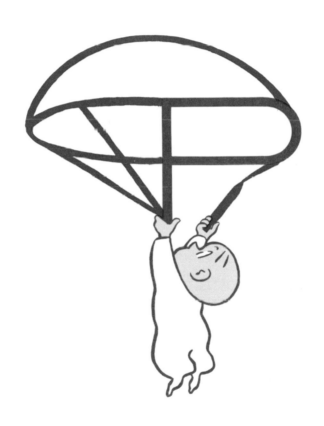

And suddenly he wondered how he could
get back over the ridge of mountains.

He would have to ask the man in the moon,
or the king, or whoever was in charge.

Q is for Queen. She was Urania, queen of
the sky, she told Harold, who bowed.

Only King Uranus could help Harold get
home, she said, but the king was away.

Far away, the queen said, across land and sea. Harold decided to ride there.

R is for Rhinoceros, roaming both land and
water.   But it was a slow rough ride.

And when Harold reached the sea, and the
next letter, he had a better idea.

S is for Sea Serpent. Harold sailed across
the moon ocean at a smooth swift speed.

He landed far away, looking for the king of
the sky who was supposed to be there.

T is for Telescope.   He set it up on a tripod.
All he saw through it was another letter.

The queen had mentioned the king's name.
Harold remembered it. U is for Uranus.

He drew the king's attention and asked how to get back across the moon mountains.

King Uranus in his ermine robe stood silent
and majestic, considering the question.

Then, with a kingly gesture, he waved Harold
forward and onward.

Harold trudged along toward another letter,
away off in the distance.

It was V for Valley.   He could go through it
to the side of the moon near the earth.

Four more letters and he would be through
the whole alphabet.

But the biggest letter of all barred his way.
He tried to think of a word for it, quickly.

W is for Witch, wicked and waiting. And it looked as if he would never get through.

Harold nearly gave up. But then he saw the
next letter, right near by.

X is for Xxxing-Out. Harold had had to X things out before, lots of times.

It worked this time too. Witches are very
susceptible to such treatment.

He had made so many marks it was hard to
get through them, but Harold managed.

Magically he found himself in a familiar
garden, with the moon high in the sky.

Y is for Yard, his own yard.   He was home!
And there was one letter left.

In his bedroom, as he dozed off, he made up a word.   Z is for Zzzl, or little snore.